school zone® publishing company

AGES 4-7

Nine Men Chase a Hen

1 LEVEL

A School Zone® Start to Read! Book

Parent Note

By the time children are ready to begin reading, they have learned about books, illustrations, and words. They know that letters make up words and words form sentences to tell stories. Much of beginning reading is memorization of words and short sentences. In order to read successfully, children need to

- master a basic vocabulary of sight words,
- learn to sound out words, and
- learn to use context clues in illustrations and text for meaning.

School Zone's Start to Read! series helps children learn to read by presenting interesting stories with easy vocabularies. Words are repeated. Sentences are short. Rhyming words help children increase their vocabulary. Meaning clues in the illustrations are abundant. After several readings with a partner, the child should be able to read alone. Most of all, the reading experience should be enjoyable.

Most of the vocabulary words in *Nine Men Chase a Hen* are typically introduced at first grade. The words *write, begin,* and *ends* are second-grade words, and the word *chase* is a higher-level word. You may need to help your child sound out these words.

ISBN 0-88743-407-X

9 780887 434075

Nine Men Chase a Hen

Written by

Barbara Gregorich

Illustrated by

John Sandford

One hen wants a hat.

Two men laugh at that.

Three men have a pet.

Four hens get very wet.

Five hens write a letter.

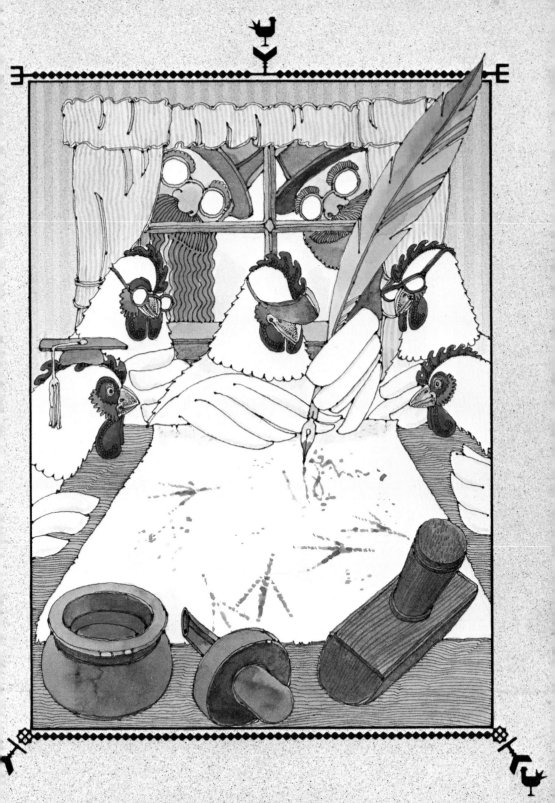

Six men say theirs is better.

Seven men sleep at night.

Eight hens make it light.

17

Nine men chase a hen.

19

Ten hens chase the men.

All the men run away.

23

All the hens begin to play.

Now this funny story ends.

All the men and hens are friends.

The End